DEAR SANTASAUR

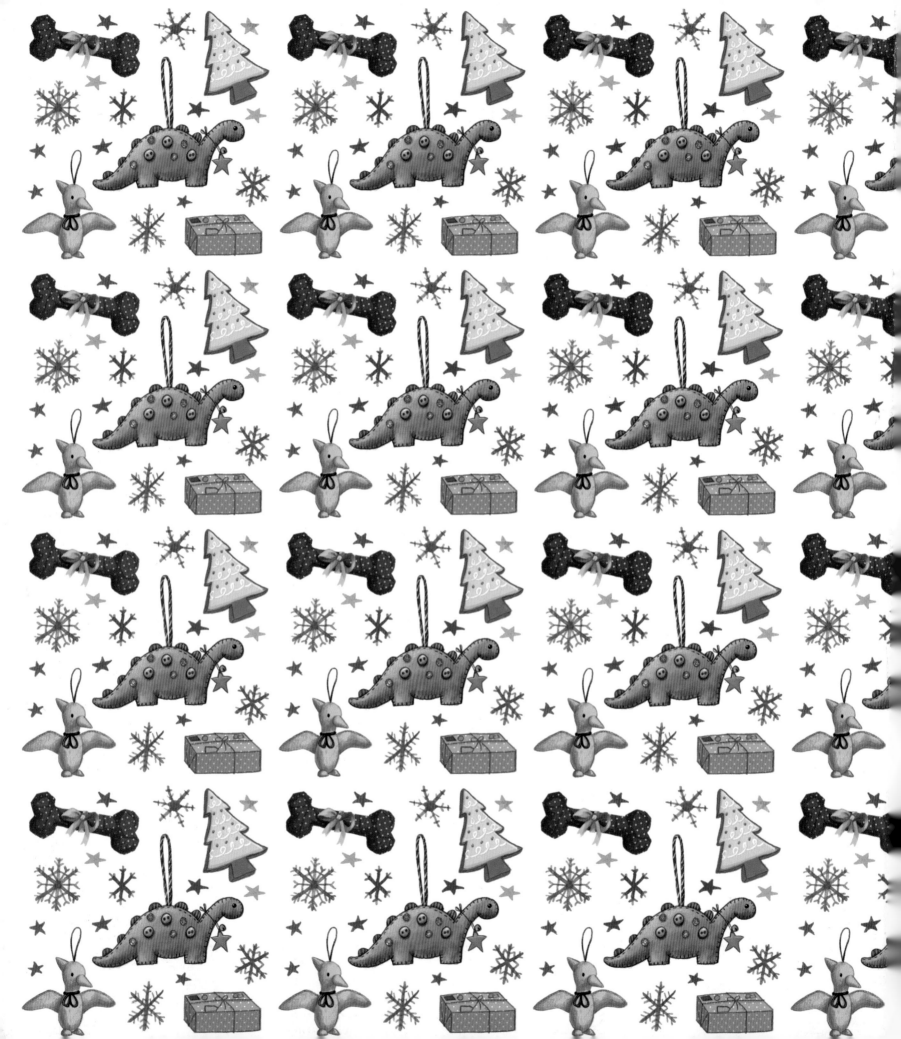

First Published in 2019 by
Scholastic Children's Books,
Euston House, 24 Eversholt Street, London NW1 1DB
a division of Scholastic Ltd

www.scholastic.co.uk
London · New York · Toronto · Sydney · Auckland
Mexico City · New Delhi · Hong Kong

With love to Little Mum's little one, Violet ~ C.S.

For Lindsosaurus and Willociraptor, with love and thanks ~ N.O.

2 3 4 5
6 7 8 9 10

DEAR
SANTASAUR

Written by
Chae
Strathie

Illustrated by
Nicola
O'Byrne

SCHOLASTIC

Max and his family were getting ready for
Christmas. Mum was writing a stack of
Christmas cards . . . and that gave Max an idea.

"Can I send a card to T.Rex at the museum?"
he asked.

"Of course you can," said Mum.

Dear Dinosaur,

MERRY CHRISTMAS!

I am helping put up decorations.
The only problem is getting the star on top of the
tree. If you were here, you might be able to reach.

Are there decorations in the Dinosaur Hall?

I am going to write my Christmas list to send to
Santa Claus tonight. Have you written yours yet?
You'd better not leave it too late!

Write back to me if you can.

Yours tinselly,

Max

x

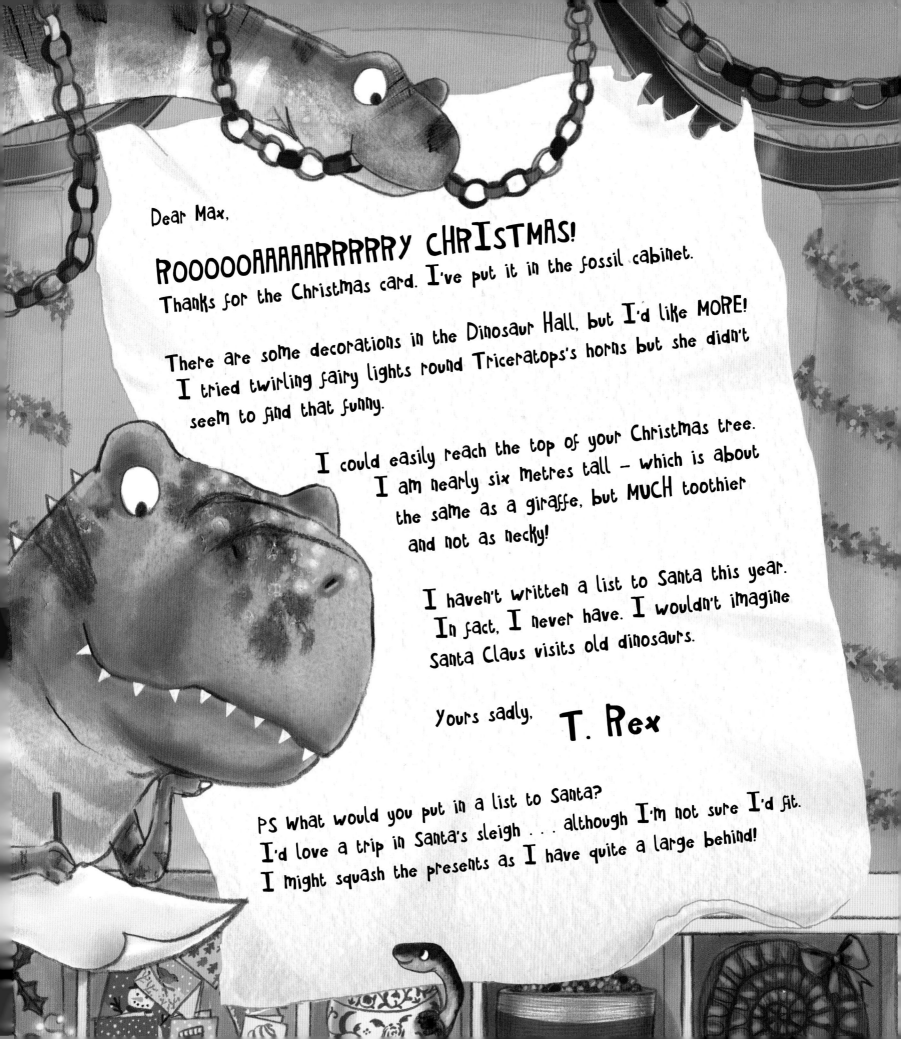

Dear Max,

ROOOOOAAAAARRRRRY CHRISTMAS!

Thanks for the Christmas card. I've put it in the fossil cabinet.

There are some decorations in the Dinosaur Hall, but I'd like MORE!
I tried twirling fairy lights round Triceratops's horns but she didn't seem to find that funny.

I could easily reach the top of your Christmas tree.
I am nearly six metres tall — which is about the same as a giraffe, but MUCH toothier and not as necky!

I haven't written a list to Santa this year. In fact, I never have. I wouldn't imagine Santa Claus visits old dinosaurs.

Yours sadly, T. Rex

PS What would you put in a list to Santa?
I'd love a trip in Santa's sleigh . . . although I'm not sure I'd fit. I might squash the presents as I have quite a large behind!

"Why doesn't Santa visit dinosaurs?" Max asked his dad.
"Perhaps his reindeer are scared of T.Rexes," said Dad.
That sounded possible to Max – after all, T.Rex did ROAR quite a lot.
But then he had a thought.

Dear Dinosaur,

Please don't be sad. Christmas is a time to be merry!

I'm sorry you've never written a list or had a visit from Santa. Maybe there is a special Santa for dinosaurs. Perhaps he is called Santa JAWS instead of Santa Claus because he is a big-mouthed T. Rex just like you!

Here's my list. Perhaps you should try writing one, too, just to see what happens.

Yours jingle bell-y,

Max X

Dear Santa,

I can't wait for Christmas Day! Have the elves been behaving? Are the reindeer full of carrots? I have been very good this year and only gave my broccoli to my dog under the table once (or maybe twice).

Here is my list:

1 - a T. Rex dressing-up costume
3 - paper and felt tip pens
5 - an invisibility cloak

2 - one million jelly beans
4 - a sleighride for my friend, T.Rex
6 - a skateboard

The most important present is the one for T.Rex.

Yours Ho-ho-hopefully,   Max X

Dear Max,

I LOVE your list.
It's very kind of you to ask for a present for me, but I don't think Santa takes MAHOOSIVE green dinosaurs for rides!

Triceratops said that Santa has a sleigh that is pulled by reindeer that can fly — and one even has a red nose! That made me laugh.

Imagine if DINOSAURS pulled Santa's sleigh. I'd like to see a red-nosed Argentinosaurus doing it. An Argentinosaurus is the longest dinosaur there is — it's even longer than a blue whale! It could pull a LOT of presents.

Here is my list:

Dear Santa,

I have been very good this year, though I did take a bite out of a model of the moon in the space exhibition. And sometimes I find it quite funny to give people a fright. I hope that's OK.

For Christmas, I would like:

1) A ride in your sleigh
2) A new fossil hunting kit for Dinosaur Dora
3) Horn glitter for Triceratops and stilts for Nanosaurus
4) A present for my friend Max
   (the T.Rex costume would be perfect)

Yours not-really-expecting-presents,

T. Rex

To: TRex@Museum.ds

Subject: Ho ho ho

Dear T. Rex,

Your list is brilliant! I hope you get everything on it.
It's very nice that you asked for presents for the others too.
Mum says being kind is what this time of year is all about.

Here is a picture of you in Santa Jaws' sleigh.

raaarhh!

Yours fingers-crossedly,

Max

x

PS Perhaps some pterosaurs could pull Santa's sleigh.
After all, they are flying reptiles and some of them were
MUCH taller than a human. They're related to birds . . .
I'm glad pigeons aren't that big. Imagine!

Max waited for
Santa to reply.

And while he
was waiting . . .

. . . it started
to SNOW.

Max built two snowmen and had a snowball fight with his friends.
But he just couldn't stop thinking about the letters he'd sent to Santa
and T.Rex.

He wished they'd hurry up and reply.

Then one morning an envelope arrived ...
with a North Pole stamp on it!

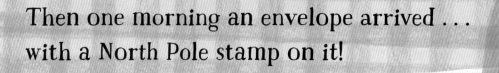

Dear Max,

Thank you very much for your letter and list.

*I think you've been acceptably good this year,
which always helps when it comes to the
whole presents thing. And I have to admit
that sometimes I give my broccoli to Rudolph.
Don't tell the elves, though, or I'll be in
big trouble.*

Roll on Christmas Eve!

Yours merrily,

Santa Claus

But that wasn't the only letter addressed
to Max in the mail that morning . . .

THE
CITY
MUSEUM
Natural History & Conservation

Dear Max,

We would like to invite you to
a fabulously festive Christmas
party for the museum's special
friends.

Come dressed in your best
dino-gear or Christmas clothes.
We're sure you'll have a
ROAR-SOME time!

Dinosaur Dora

MIDDLE STREET SQUARE · GREENVILLE · DN0 5AR

Dad said he's **not very good**
at making things so he
took us to the costume shop.

| Send | Attach | Address | Fonts | Draft |

To: TRex@Museum.ds

Subject: Party time!

Dear T. Rex

HOORAY! It arrived! Santa wrote a letter back to me.

And not only that, I got an invitation to a party at

the museum as well. That means I'll see you soon.

Max

X

Dear Max,

I'm not sure if Santa Claus (or Santa JAWS) got my list, but I don't mind.

We had a snowball fight after the visitors went home, but Nanosaurus went in a huff because my snowballs were bigger than he is and he kept disappearing. Then we built a snowdino with carrots for teeth! Ha ha!

Have a very merry and magical Christmas. I can't wait to see you on Boxing Day.

Yours snowily,

T. Rex

When Christmas morning arrived Max could hardly contain his excitement.
Santa had **been**, and he'd delivered all the presents Max had asked for.
Well, almost all . . .
He'd even left Max a note.

"Do you think T.Rex really got a ride in Santa's sleigh after all?" gasped Max.

Dear Max,
Your friend T.Rex and I had a marvellous time last night.
He was VERY helpful.
Who knew dinosaurs could be so much fun?
(Although he did squash some presents – he has a rather large bottom, you see.)
Yours beardily,
Santa Claus

"I don't think Santa has time to take dinosaurs for a whirl on Christmas Eve!" laughed his mum.

When Max and his family arrived at the museum on Boxing Day the party was already in full swing. Dinosaur Dora was there to greet them.

"Merry Christmas!" she said. "The dinosaurs got some very interesting presents yesterday.

Merry Christmas

Nanosaurus is much taller than usual . . .
Triceratops looks wonderfully sparkly . . .

and T.Rex . . .

Dear T. Rex,

Thank you for all your **roarsome** help on Christmas Eve!

Love, *Santa* x

Santa's Little Helper!

. . . seems VERY pleased with himself."

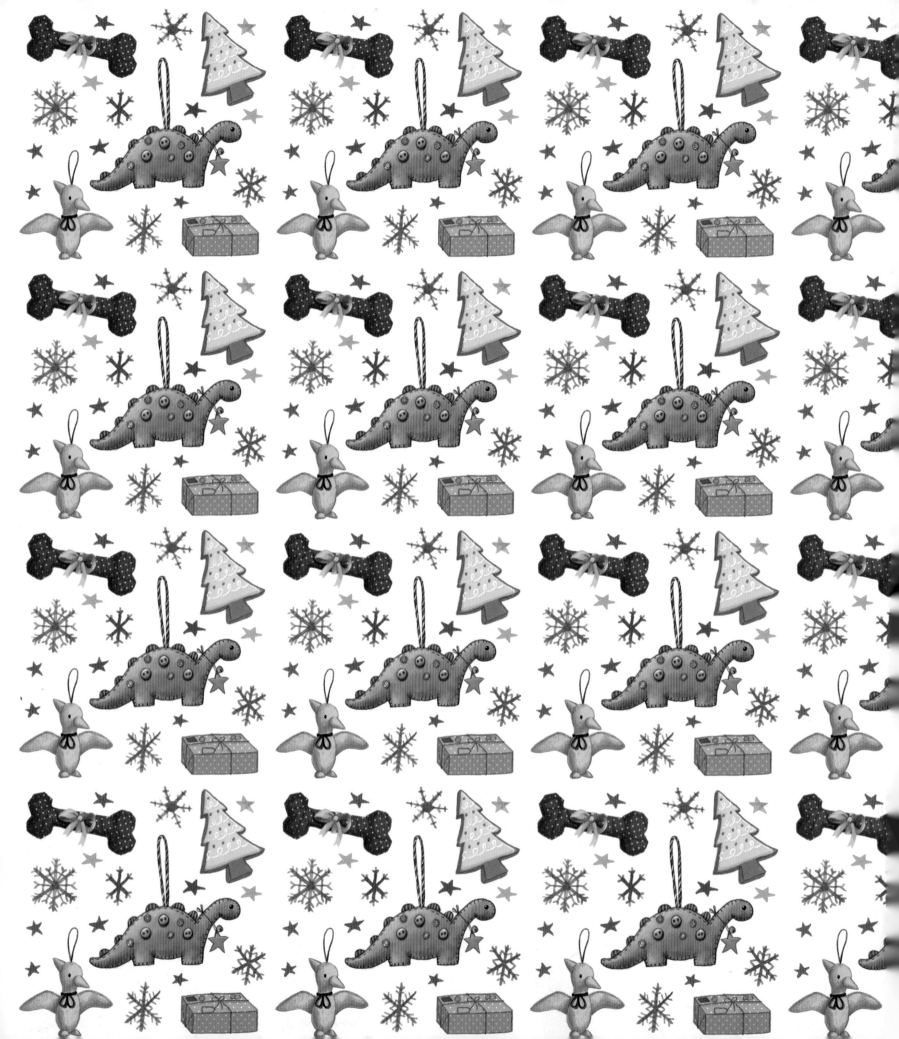